Loving the Bratva

K.D Clark

Published by K.D Clark, 2021.

www.kdclarkpublishing.com

Loving the Bratva
K.D Clark

Sign up for my newsletter to stay up to date on all new releases. https://kdclark926116107.wpcomstaging.com/newsletter/

ALSO BY K.D CLARK

Merciless Queen

Twisted Judgement

Apprehension

Savage Spades

Dirty Empire

King of The Bronx

Escaping the Bratva

Hating the Bratva

Loving the Bratva

Penthouse Heist

Zeke:Before Dishonor

Golden Handcuffs

Carmen

I grab Maven's hand and lead him across the main floor, switching my hips as I walk. He slaps hands with some members of the Motown gang, and they hoot, holler, and pat him on the back. I try not to roll my eyes. He paid for a private session with me. Even though I hate these assholes in my brother's gang, it's good money, and I could use that right now.

Once we turn the corner, there's a long hallway with a private room at the end. I turn the sign over that's hanging on the front of the door, notifying the other girls that it's occupied. I open the door and wave Maven inside. I can feel the cold draft that's always present in this room because there's another door that leads out to the back parking lot. I try not to shiver as the cool air drifts across my exposed skin.

"Take a seat," I say, keeping my voice low and sultry.

That's what men like. It's all an act. Most of this job is; pretending that I'm aroused by the pure thought of men ogling me as I dance. He sits down on the tacky purple couch that looks like it was placed here in the 70's. I try not to think about the dirt and human fluids that have sunk into the cushions over the years. I close the door and dim the lights. Maven runs a tongue over his bottom lip. His eyes are low and heavy, like he's had way too much to drink. He's new to the club. The Motown gang runs the strip club, so I know nearly everyone. Maven showed up several months ago, and it's obvious he's an outsider. With skin white as snow in the middle of Detroit, he sticks out like a sore thumb.

I press a button on the old CD player, and soft music fills the air. It can barely be heard over the loud music outside the door, but it will do.

I run a hand through my long caramel hair, making sure to exaggerate the movement before I start to dance. Maven shifts in his seat. He paid for an hour, that's one-hundred dollars in my pocket if I can keep him entertained. The key is to dance really slow and take as long as possible to take my clothes off because once they're off...well, they're off, and I have no desire to spend more than fifteen minutes naked in front of this man. His dick grows hard against his jeans. As I dance, he keeps adjusting himself.

When I'm down to just my bra and panties, I straddle him. His hands run over my thighs, and I allow him to touch me. The men aren't supposed to touch us, that's the rule. But, rules get broken, and when they do, it usually means more money. If he touched me anywhere besides my thighs, then I'd put him in his place. I would never sleep with any of these men. That's too far. I'm here to dance and that's it.

His head falls back on the couch as I move my hips against the bulge in his jeans. Maven is good-looking, which makes my job a lot easier. It's hard to stomach dancing for some of the guys that come in here.

Maven opens his mouth like he's about to say something when the door behind me bursts open. I let out a yell before jumping up from Maven's lap. I turn around just fast enough to get a look at the intruder. I thought it might be Justin, or one of the guys playing a prank, or maybe even a drunk customer who somehow wandered his way outside and was trying to get back in. The man in front of me is neither of those. Even in my heels, he towers over me. His body takes up a massive amount of space in the small private dancing room. His dark eyes flicker to me briefly before narrowing on my customer.

"Oh shit!" Maven yelps, struggling to stand on his drunken feet.

The monster of a man rushes towards him, pulls out a gun, and hits Maven over the head with it. His body slumps to the grimy tile floor. I'm too stunned to scream, to run, to do anything. I stand there frozen as the man picks Maven up like a sack of potatoes and slings him over his shoulder.

He doesn't even glance at me as he walks back out the door. My heart hammers almost on beat to the music on the other side of the closed door that leads out to a hallway and eventually turns into the main strip area. Run Carmen, the voice in my head screams at me. I have to tell someone what happened. How the fuck am I supposed to explain that I went into a private room with Maven, and he was attacked and kidnapped by a monster. Run! The voice in my head screams again. It's enough to make me snap out of my trance. I dash to the door and turn the handle, but it doesn't budge. What the hell? I try again. Nothing.

"It's blocked," a rough, gravelly voice says from behind me. A chill runs over my body. His shoes squeak on the floor, and I turn so fast my hair hits me across the face.

He has stubbles across his square jawline. His eyes are dark, cold, and empty. Like there is no more softness left in him. Pure evil stares back at me. I've seen that emptiness before. Some of the Motown gang members have seen stuff that no person should ever see, and afterward, it's like their soul changes form. As if their soul couldn't deal with what was witnessed and ultimately leaves their body. That same look is present in this man. I've never felt so small in my life.

"Please," I whisper. I don't know why he's here or why he took Maven, and I don't care. I need to make it out of this room.

He takes a step closer, and something in me snaps. I pound my hand against the red wooden door.

"Help! Help!" I scream, hoping someone might be in the hallway and can hear me. He covers my mouth, and I twist and turn against his hold.

"Would you calm the fuck down," he grunts, trying to get me under control, but I slap and claw at any piece of skin I can land my hand on.

I want to hurt him. If I can hurt him, then I can run, but my opportunity doesn't last long. He manages to cross my arms over my chest and force me to sit down on the couch. My chest heaves as I stare up at him. The only sound in the room is the thudding of the music that's too fucking loud.

"Let me go," I seethe.

He smirks, something I didn't think this man would be capable of. With one hand still keeping me pinned to the couch, he uses his other hand to dig in his pocket. My heart skips a beat, but it starts up again when I realize it's only his wallet. He manages to dig out some cash and lays it on the cushion next to me.

"When I let you go," he says, his voice surprisingly calm. "Take this money, leave and never come back here again. You didn't see anything. You didn't hear anything. Got it?"

I nod like a bobblehead. He's not going to kill me.

He lifts an eyebrow. That smirk is still on his handsome face like he finds me amusing. Up close, I can see how attractive he is. Even with those dark, soulless eyes, he's still a ridiculously gorgeous man.

He lets me go and leaves just as fast as he barged in.

*****

"You don't have to work tonight?" Sierra asks me as she flips through a stack of mail. She frowns as she lifts an overdue water bill.

"No, I got a big tipper a couple of weeks ago so I can take some time off." The lie leaves my tongue easily because I knew she'd ask me why I've been hanging around the house more lately. Usually, I sleep until one or two in the afternoon, but I've been up bright and early these last couple of weeks.

She drops the mail in the center of the wooden kitchen table where I'm sitting before raising an eyebrow at me.

"Big tipper?"

Sierra and I grew up almost like twins. She's a couple years older than me, but once our brother, Ruthless, took over the Motown gang, we stuck together. We needed to in order to survive because our dad would be rolling in his grave if he knew Ruthless completely shut us out. We've managed to stay above water independently, but the goal is always to leave Detroit behind. There's nothing for us here besides memories, no jobs, no opportunities...nothing.

"Yeah, older creepy guy. Hey, do you have some quarters I can borrow?" I ask, trying desperately to change the subject. Sierra's overprotective of me, and I guess I can understand why.

We live in one of the most dangerous cities in the United States, and I work in a strip club. She threw a fit when she found out where I was working, but we needed the money. Ruthless doesn't even seem to care that his little sister shakes her naked body in front of men in his gang. He's different now.

Sierra grabs her purse from off the hook and digs around. Strands of hair from her big, curly afro fall in front of her face as she searches. A few seconds later, she comes up with a hand full of quarters. She drops them in my palm before sliding the messenger bag over her body. The resemblance between us is uncanny. We both have the same light brown skin tone, full lips, and high cheekbones. Dad used to say we got all of mom's good looks. The only way people can usually tell the difference between us is our hair. While Sierra keeps her natural curls, I choose to wear mine straight.

"I should probably get running. The bus came early yesterday, and I almost missed it. I'll see you for dinner?"

I nod. "Yep."

Once I hear the front door shut. I reach in the pocket of my sweatpants and pull out the cash. I count it out. Two hundred dollars. That's all I have left from the man who could have easily taken my life. He left me a grand, and I used it to catch up on all the bills I could, now I'll have to go back to the club.

Take this money, leave and never come back here again.

The memory of his words sends a shiver down my spine. He warned me not to come back, but I don't have much of a choice. The bright orange letter in front of me from the sewage company read; OVERDUE. One day I'll be able to escape this endless cycle of just scraping by, but I have no idea when.

I manage to close the front door while balancing the mesh laundry bag in my arms. Once it's closed and locked, I drop the laundry bag on top of the other pile of clothes inside the wheeled basket. It would be nice if our apartment came with laundry, but of course not. Double checking that I have everything I need, including my gun tucked inside my backpack, I head towards the laundry mat. Luckily it's only a few blocks away from us, so I don't have to get on the push with all this shit. Since it's still early in the morning, I'm not scared of walking alone. Everyone is mostly asleep in the neighborhood until about two o'clock or so. I pass by overgrown lawns, abandoned houses, empty lots, and boarded up businesses before getting to the laundromat. I'm relieved to see that it's empty. I throw in a couple of loads before relaxing back in one of the plastic chairs. Pulling out the notebook and pen from my bag, I start to write. I haven't told anyone about my writing yet, but it's the best part of my day. It's the only time when I can pretend I'm somewhere else. I can pretend that I graduated from college and moved far, far away from Detroit. I was able to find a good-paying job and move my sister with me. All the characters and stories I write are my fantasies, and one day I'll make them a reality.

Xavier

Maven whimpers as I slam his heavy ass onto the metal table in the middle of the clubhouse basement. It's been a long-ass car ride with this asshole from Detroit to Boston. He begged and pleaded for miles until I shoved a gag in his mouth and threw his ass in the trunk. I didn't feel sorry for the guy one bit. He's been working with the Motown gang behind our back. He was stupid to think they could protect him from me. I can get in and out of places without a trace if I need to...except this time. This time I left a witness.

An image of the woman I left behind pops in my head. She was perfect, not like the girls in Boston who were all starting to look a little too cookie-cutter for me. Her big brown eyes gave away her fear, but I could tell that she was studying me. I should have killed her. I've never hesitated to kill a witness before, but something about her made me stop. She didn't belong in the back of a strip club giving lap dances to scum like Maven.

"Xavier, listen to me I didn't tell them anything," Maven pleads, and I'm snapped back to the present. He's managed to get his gag off while I've been daydreaming. That woman is already causing me trouble. I never take my eyes off my target. I slam my open palm into his chest, making him lay flat on the table. There's a meeting going on upstairs that I wanted to make it to, but I came in too damn late. Now I'll have to get the play-by-play from someone else. I use the straps attached to the table to hold Maven down as he continues to try to convince me he did nothing wrong. Once I'm done, I pull a chair up beside him. Underneath the table is a second shelf holding all the weapons someone might need to torture. I'm not a big fan of torture. I'd rather kill someone and get it over with. Hearing someone beg and plead for their life isn't my cup of tea.

"What did you tell them, Maven?" I ask.

He drops his head to the table, accepting his fate. He'll never make it out of this basement, and he knows it.

"I didn't tell them anything about the brotherhood."

"Then why were you there?"

"I helped them move some extra weight; heroin mostly. That's what I wanted to do for the brotherhood, but Gavrill wouldn't let me move. Said that I had to work my way out. It's bullshit-"

"No, what's bullshit is you going behind the back of the entire Bratva and teaming up with someone else because you think you're better than us. You don't think anyone else has been assigned a job they hate?"

Maven doesn't say anything.

With a sigh, I stand to my feet and grab the screwdriver from underneath the table. I stand over Maven as I ask the question, "Now, what did you tell them?"

"I told you I-"

I jam the screwdriver right into his upper thigh. Before he can scream, I stuff a dirty washcloth in his mouth. His scream comes out harsh and gargled.

"Has he said anything yet?" I look up to see that Alek has made his way to the basement. Thank god, I don't feel like dealing with this asshole all night.

I shake my head. "Just got started. I found him in a private room at a strip club. The other men were too far away to hear me, but I'm sure they know now."

"What did you do with the stripper?" he asks. Fuck, I shouldn't have said anything about the private strip room. Alek is in line to become Pakhan, and part of the reason he made it to this point is that he doesn't fuck around. He likes business to be cut, dry, and clean. Anyone who steps out of line, in his eyes, needs to go.

"Xavier?" he asks again. I could lie and say I killed her, but he'd find out, and I don't have any desire to end up like Maven.

"I gave her some cash. Told her she didn't see anything."

He narrows his eyes at me. "Get your ass back there. We don't leave witnesses."

"She's not a threat." Not that Alek would care. The woman was terrified, and I gave her enough money, so hopefully, she'd stay away from the strip club as I told her to. She'll get another job, realize how dangerous it is.

"Bullshit. Did she see your face?"

I don't say anything because, yeah, she saw my face. She stared into my eyes as if she could read everything beneath the cold, hard surface.

"That's what I thought."

Maven moans on the table. Alek grabs the handle of the screwdriver and twists it. Maven screams into the dirty washcloth. "Can't you see we're having a conversation here?"

Maven's eyes start to roll back, and Alek slaps his cheek. "Hey, not yet. We have a long day ahead of us."

Alek turns his attention back to me. "Go back and take care of that fucking stripper."

I turn my back on Alek and walk the way I came out of the basement. I take the concrete steps up to the parking lot where Alyona stands guard.

"Didn't want to stay around?" he asks me, having seen me drag Maven down to the basement.

I shake my head. "Looks like my job isn't over."

"Shit, you have to go back?" he asks, adjusting the rifle that's slung across his chest. "Tell me you're at least flying this time?"

I almost laughed. "Fuck yeah, I'm flying."

We hear a scream from behind us, and Alyona chuckles. "He should have just been patient. Gavrill would have agreed to move him to another position after a while."

I shake my head. "Some people are just fucking stupid."

Alyona slaps me on the back. "I have to do a round but have a safe trip. Don't fuck this one up. We haven't seen you around in a while."

He's right. It seems like lately, I've had one job right after another. Always either saving someone or taking someone out. I can't complain; I love what I do. I couldn't ask for a better job within the brotherhood. Alyona heads the other way while I walk to my hummer in the parking lot. As I pull out of the parking lot and head towards my house, I can't stop thinking about what I'm going to have to do. I can't disobey a direct order. Even though Alek isn't Pakhan yet, he might as well be. Gavrill has taken more of a backseat lately. I've never had a problem getting rid of an enemy, but I have a feeling deep in my gut that this one is going to be different.

Carmen

I wipe my sweaty palms on my leggings before opening the door to the strip club. I managed to hold out two more days before coming back to this place, but I'm all out of money, and the job market in Detroit is non-existent. The jobs that are available pay so bad we could barely cover rent. The main floor is pretty much empty since the club doesn't open for another hour. The room is dark except for the stage and floor lights that are still on.

"Carmen?"

I turn towards the bar, where Jessica is pouring herself a drink.

"Where the hell have you been?"

Jessica is pretty, with long blonde hair and blue eyes. Her stripper name is Snow Bunny, for obvious reasons.

I adjust my duffle bag on my shoulder before walking over to her. "I needed some time off," I say, offering the lame excuse.

She takes a sip of her drink which looks like a mix of Vodka and Red Bull. "I hear you there. I need a break too. I worked five nights last week."

"Damn, girl."

She shrugs. "It's worth it for the money. I'm just trying to save up, so I never have to come back here."

I nod. "I feel you on that."

She takes another drink and leans closer to me. "Ruthless has been asking about you."

I frown. "I'm sure he has."

I knew I'd have to offer some kind of explanation as to why Maven and I both went missing the same night. I tried to think of a good lie, but lying to my brother would only dig a deeper hole between our already fractured relationship. I had to come out and tell him the truth. The threat that the mystery man left me with hangs over my head, but I have to go back to my life. I can't hide out at my house, scared for the rest of my life.

"Carmen!" I jump at the deep voice. Justin, Ruthless's guard dog, is coming towards me.

"I can hear just fine, Justin. You can lower your voice," I snap. I try my best to hold my tongue around here, but Justin seems to always rub me the wrong way. He smiles at me, amused by my attitude.

Jessica downs the rest of her drink. "Well, I'm going to get ready. I'll see you in the dressing room?" she asks me.

"Yep."

She walks across the floor towards the backroom. Justin waits until she's gone before stepping close to me.

"Where have you been?" he asks, the smell of weed coming off him in waves.

I cross my arms over my chest. "I was at home."

"You didn't tell anyone you were taking time off. It's weird...Maven disappeared too."

"Is there something you want?"

"Boss wants to talk with you."

I uncross my arms and walk around Justin towards the office. "That's all you had to say," I grumble.

Even though I can't stand my brother, I much rather talk to him than his stupid, annoying guard dog. I don't bother knocking on the door before opening it. When I realize what

I'm looking at, I wish I had knocked. My brother is leaned back in the office chair, his eyes closed, while Red, one of the strippers, is on her knees in front of him.

"Oh...fuck...sorry," I quickly close the door but not before I see Ruthless open his eyes and snare at me.

Justin laughs from behind me.

"You could have warned me!"

He shrugs. "Nah, that was more fun."

"If he needs me, he can come find me. I'll be in the dressing room." I flip Justin the bird while walking away.

It doesn't take long for Ruthless to stroll into the dressing room with Red on his heels. She holds her head high as if it's some kind of status symbol to suck my brother off. My stomach turns at just the thought. She goes to her locker to get ready for the night while Ruthless walks up to me.

"We need to talk," he says slowly, looking at me from under slightly hooded eyelids. He's high, but he always is now. Ruthless has always had this slow, quiet, calmness about him that makes him dangerous in this kind of business. Justin handles anything that requires punishment or threats, but Ruthless is the brains behind the operation. I don't think most people realize just how intelligent Ruthless is. Behind his calm demeanor is the same kid that spent hours with his nose in a book way above his reading level.

He tilts his head, and I follow him to a corner of the dressing room where the other girls can't over hear us.

"What happened to Maven?" he asks. "Last time anyone saw him was with you, heading to a private dance."

I nervously run a hand through the long waves I just put in my hair with the flat iron.

"Tell me what happened, Carmen. He hurt you?"

When he asks something like that, I can almost believe he cares about me. But I remind myself that Ruthless doesn't care about anyone besides himself anymore.

"No. While I was dancing, some guy barged in through the outside door. Big guy, built like Hercules or some shit. He took Maven."

Ruthless doesn't change his facial expression at the news, and I realize it's because he already knows. He was testing me, seeing if I would be honest. I ball my hands into a fist.

"Really? You knew what happened, and you didn't even see if I was okay?" It takes everything I have not to shove him away from me.

Out of habit, he runs his hand over the waves indented into his short hair. While Sierra and I could be twins, Ruthless looks a lot like our father, with dark skin, light brown eyes, and muscle definition that he grew from being an athlete in high school and managed to maintain. It's easy to see why the other strippers fall all over him.

"It's nothing personal," he says.

"I'm your sister. It is personal!"

It's bad enough that he's okay with me working in the strip club. My father would be embarrassed if he could see the man Ruthless turned into.

"Have a good night," Is all he offers before leaving the dressing room.

After spending the next hour applying my makeup, putting on my lingerie, and making sure I looked my best, I head out to the main floor. I pull my shoulders back and muster up all the confidence I can. The main floor is packed from person to person. Saturday nights are usually the busiest. Normally I'd be happy because a busy club means I'll go home with a bra full of money, but I can't shake the bad feeling in my stomach. Red is on stage doing her routine. Men closest to the stage throw money and hoop and holler. The music is so loud I can barely hear myself think, let alone make out whatever disgusting thing they're saying. The darkness of the club adds to the ambiance. It took three months of working before I could walk the floor in my heels without embarrassing myself. I have an hour or so before it's my turn to get on stage, so I walk around the floor. I can feel eyes on me as I weave through the tables making sure to sway my hips as I do. After a couple of lap dances on the floor, Joey, the club manager, comes over to me.

"There's a man asking specifically for you. One-hundred dollars for a dance."

"Where is he?"

Joey tilts his head to a table in the corner. I can barely see the man since he's hidden in the shadows. The tables are more spread out over there. He's wearing a dark jacket with the hood up.

I swallow. "Okay."

That sick feeling in my stomach seems to intensify, but I can't let that feeling overtake me. I have to get through the night.

The music increases, and I look to see that Jessica has now taken the stage. All eyes turn to her, and I continue to walk towards the man. He's sitting in the chair with his legs spread open. His large frame takes up the entire seat. These chairs weren't built for men his size. The hundred-dollar bill sits on the table next to him.

"Hey handsome, I heard you've been asking for me," I say in a voice so fake I barely recognize it myself. He grunts in response and pushes a hundred dollar bill towards me. What a fucking weirdo. We get guys like this sometimes. I roll my eyes before taking the hundred-dollar bill and tucking it into my bra. I place both hands on his shoulders, slightly rubbing into his rigid muscles before I start to dance. I feel his eyes all over me even though I can't see his face with the combination of the hoodie and the dark corner. I draw my hands down and run them over his denim-covered legs. His muscles bunch underneath my touch as I drop into a deep squat.

He's made of pure muscle. I make my way back up his body and straddle him. I can feel his hard dick through the thin lace of my panties. I'm used to men having a boner pretty much the entire time they're here, but he feels more prominent than average. What is a man like this doing in a strip club? I grind against him, and his fingers dig in my thighs. I don't always allow men to touch me this much, but there's something pleasurable about the way he does it. He wraps his arms around my waist, and panic starts to take over as he squeezes my body close to his.

"Hey, what-"

He leans forward and growls in my ear. "I thought I told you never to come back here."

Carmen

I freeze. Time seems to slow as realization washes over me. It feels like my heart stops for a moment. He tilts his head back, and the hoodie falls. Those same dark, soulless eyes are staring at me. The same ones that I saw in the private dance room. He warned me. He warned me not to come back. Now what? I try to stand, but he still has me around the waist.

"What do you want?"

"I paid for a dance."

"I'll scream," I warn.

He pulls a wad of money out of his jacket pocket and slaps it down on the table.

"Finish the dance."

I stare into his eyes, trying to get a read on him. The money on the table calls to me. I feel used, dirty because I know I don't have the luxury to walk away from that much money. So I decide to dance, despite the questions that are swimming around in my head. He loosens his grip around my waist enough that I can stand again. I glance at the clock on the wall. He paid for an hour, which means I still have thirty minutes left. I do my usual routine, keeping my eye on the clock as I do so. The time seems to slow down the more I wish it would speed up. His eyes never leave mine even when I take off my top, letting my breasts fall free.

As soon as our time is up, I quickly put my bra back on and snatch the roll of money off the table. He grabs my arm before I can walk off.

"That's more money than you would make in a week. You're done dancing for the night. Go home."

"That's not how it works, big guy." I tear my arm from his grip and walk across the floor to the dressing room. I'm relieved to see that it's empty. All the other girls are out on the floor. I unlock my locker to shove the money inside. I pause and decide to count it, two thousand dollars. He gave me two thousand dollars for an hour-long dance. He wasn't wrong when he said it's more than I'd make in a week.

"Carmen," a voice says from behind me, and I quickly tuck the money into my bag in the locker, just as Joey comes around the corner.

"You can go home for the night."

I raise an eyebrow at him. "Why?"

"Do you want the rest of the night off or what?" he snaps before turning his back to me and walking out of the dressing room.

What the hell is going on? Joey never wants us to leave early. The more girls on the floor means more money for the club. Especially if one of the customers gets attached to a certain girl, they'll keep coming back to see her. I don't let myself dawn on the weirdness of this situation any longer. I grab my stuff before he can change his mind and leave.

When I get home, the living room light is still on. I double-check my phone, forgetting just how early it is. I'm usually never home before three am, and if it's a really good night, sometimes I don't get back until five. I unlock the door and turn to see Sierra curled up on the couch with a book in her hand. It's one of those mystery books, the same ones our mom used to read when we were kids.

"Hey, you're early," Sierra says, checking her watch.

"I know I...um got off early."

"That's nice?" she asks. Fewer hours on the floor usually means less money. I could continue to lie to her, but I tell Sierra everything, and keeping this monster man a secret doesn't sit right with me.

I drop my bag and sit on the recliner across from her.

"I have to tell you something. I should have told you before, but I didn't think it would turn into anything."

She sets her book down and focuses all her attention on me. She reminds me so much of Mom when she does that. Sierra inherited all those good traits from her; kind, patient, helpful. Not me. Me and Ruthless happen to inherit our traits from our father. He was a good father, but his focus was always money. How to make more, how to spend it, how to keep it in the family, etc. He worked so much I don't even remember him that well.

"What is it, Carmen?" Sierra asks, breaking my train of thought.

I take a deep breath before launching into the story. I tell her about the night that I watched Maven be carried away from the club. How this man told me not to come back and about tonight when he had me dance for him. I also make sure to mention that Ruthless knew about the whole thing and didn't even check on me.

"What does he want?"

I throw my hands up. "How should I know?"

"Did he tell you not to come back again?"

I shrug. "No, but he basically tried to tell me that my shift was over. I let him know that's not how it works, but then Joey told me I could go home. Any other night I would argue, but since that man already gave me this," I reach in my pocket and throw her the roll of money. She catches it with wide eyes. "I figured there was no point in staying."

Sierra rolls the money around in her hands. "I don't like this. What kind of person has this kind of money on them to give to a stripper...no offense."

I slap a hand over my chest. "A stripper? I'm an exotic dancer."

She rolls her eyes. "Are you going to go back tomorrow?"

I nod.

"And what if he comes back?"

I shake my head. "Then I'll take more of his money."

"Carmen!"

"What?"

"This is creepy. What if the guy is like stalking you?"

I get up from the recliner to sit next to her on the couch. "I'll be fine. I promise."

A moment of silence passes between us as we both get lost in our thoughts.

"What doesn't make sense about all this is why Ruthless would let him inside the club for a second time. The club is swarming with men in the Motown Gang. Ruthless had to know your mystery man was there tonight. After he took Maven, he shouldn't have been able to get through the door."

She means to say that Ruthless should have shot the man as soon as he approached the club. Ruthless might not give a shit about us, but he cares about his precious gang, and he's not one to tolerate disrespect.

"That is weird. You think I should ask Ruthless?"

Sierra shrugs. "If you can get an answer, why not?"

Yeah, that would be the real problem—Ruthless answers to no one.

"Do you want some hot chocolate?" Sierra asks, unfolding herself from the couch.

"You need to get a man."

She waves me off, and I follow her into the kitchen. "What do I need a man for? To move in here and mess up everything?"

"Not all men are low-lives."

She huffs. "That's all that's around here."

She opens the cabinet and begins to make two cups of hot chocolate even though I hadn't answered her question.

"Well then, maybe we should leave," I say quietly.

"Yeah, as soon as we can afford it. Detroit is cheap, and if we can't afford to live here, we can't afford to live somewhere else."

"But there's more opportunities somewhere else. Maybe we can find something better that way I don't have to shake my ass for those fuckers."

She gives me a sad smile.

"Maybe I can get a job at an office or something," I say.

This time she laughs before going back to making the drinks.

"What?"

"You would not survive in an office. You think you can sit at a desk for eight hours a day?"

I smirk at the thought. She's right. I can do a lot of things but being stuck in a cubicle isn't my style, but I'd suffer through it if it meant we could get out of Detroit. She hands me the cup.

"I think I'm going to watch some TV before going to bed. Want to join me?"

I shake my head. "I'm going to write for a little bit."

"Alright, I'll see you in the morning?"

"Maybe."

I take my cup and bag down the hall to my bedroom. After taking a shower and getting settled, I open my notebook and get to work.

*****

The club is already packed when I get there. The night is in full swing as I make my way to the dressing room. I've been nervous since the moment I woke up. My mystery man gave me enough money for weeks worth of work. He probably expects me to take the money and stay away. But I don't scare that easily. I walk out of the dressing room after changing into my outfit for the night and nearly run into Justin.

"What?" I ask, not in the mood for his bullshit this early into my shift.

"Private dance."

I throw my hands up. "I just got here."

He winks. "Congrats."

He turns around to leave, but I grab him by the shirt.

"What the fuck," he snaps, moving out of my hold.

"Why did Joey let me go home last night?"

He smiles, showing off those two gold teeth in his mouth that makes me cringe. "Why do you think?"

I take a deep breath. "Did that guy...the one I was dancing with tell you-"

"No one tells me shit. Why Joey sent you home is club business." He walks away. "Don't keep your client waiting," he says before turning the corner.

I clench my hands into fists. I don't know why I bothered asking him. I knew I wouldn't get a serious answer. I take a deep breath and try to put on my happy face before going to the private room. I open the door, and that happy face instantly falls as I spot the mystery man sitting on the couch.

His elbows rest on his knees in that man-spread pose guys do. He was typing something on his phone but looks up when I walk in. For the first time, I realize how handsome he is. His eyes aren't so dark today, and I wonder what that means.

The first time I saw him, I was scared for my life, and the second time he was hidden by the shadows. Those aren't the best opportunities to get a good look at someone but, I'm getting my chance now. He's dressed in a pair of dark jeans and a plain black t-shirt. A single gold chain hangs around his neck, and for a moment, I picture that necklace dangling over me. Where the hell did that thought come from? He leans back on the couch and tucks his phone in his pocket, giving me his full attention.

I close the door and walk further into the room. I stand in front of him with my arms crossed over my chest.

He raises an eyebrow. "Aren't you going to dance?"

"No, I'm not going to dance," I sputter. "Why are you here?"

"I paid for a dance."

"Yeah, well, I have questions."

"Dance, and I'll answer your questions."

He looks at me, waiting. What the hell is wrong with this guy?

"Fine," I grit out. "Why are you here?"

He leans over and pushes the play button on the old CD player. A song I recognize plays through the speakers, and he tilts his head towards me.

I run a hand through my hair, trying to get my anger in check, and then I start to dance. He watches me, his eyes lowering with desire.

"I asked a question," I remind him, not missing a step in my routine.

"What was the question?"

I roll my eyes. "Why are you here?"

"Easy, I'm here for the dance."

I'm going to strangle this man.

"I'm here for you," he clarifies.

I pause. "For me? Why? What do you want from me?"

He waves me on. Clenching my teeth together, I continue my routine. "Yes, for you, because you witnessed something you weren't supposed to witness, and I'm not sure what I want from you yet."

His eyes roam over my body as he says the last sentence. But he's not looking at me like other men do. It's not in a 'you're just a sex object' kind of way. No, he's looking at me with pure admiration, like he's impressed by the way my body can move. After working here so long, I forget that, unlike the other girls, I have training. When I was a young girl, Mom put me in dance classes as soon as I could walk. I continued up until college. I missed it a lot when I was in school. After I dropped out and Sierra told me about how Ruthless took over the MoTown gang, I was too broke to even think about going back. I'd lost my father and brother in one go.

"Who are you?" I ask, focusing back on the task at hand. I need information from him. Knowledge is power.

"Finally, a question worth something. My name's Xavier."

I take off my first piece of clothing. The silk robe I'm wearing is tossed across the floor. He shifts in his seat, and something about the movement makes me feel accomplished, like I'm somehow winning whatever game this is he's playing with me.

"Ok, Xavier...anything else?"

"That's not a question," he replies.

"Where are you from?" I pick up on the hint of an accent, but I can't place it. He does an excellent job of hiding it.

"Boston, grew up in a Russian household. That's the question you're really asking."

I grip the couch behind his head and move my hips from side to side. My tits are right up to his face. If he leaned forward, he'd be in my bra.

"Why does my brother let you back in here?"

His eyes stay trained on my face even though my breasts are an inch away from him.

"Because he'd be stupid to start a conflict between our organizations."

"What organizations?"

He smirks. "The Russian mafia and the Motown gang. We're not allies by any means, but we aren't enemies either...at least not yet."

I let his words sink in as I straddle his hips. I place his hands on my waist, allowing him to feel my skin. I don't know much about the Russian mafia. Maybe I should be more afraid than

I am, but you start to become immune to it when you grow up around organized criminal activity.

"You aren't even fazed," he comments. His dick grows underneath me.

"Why would I be?" I reach behind me to unclasp my bra, but he stops me. He grips my waist harder and flips me over so fast I barely have time to register what happened. I'm on the couch in the spot he was sitting, and he's standing over me. He grabs his wallet and pulls out a roll of money, just like the night before.

"Have a good night, Carmen," he says before leaving me alone in the room. It takes me a minute to recover and realize what he just said; Carmen. *How the fuck does he know my name?*

Xavier

"I don't think any jobs are waiting for you, so you're all good," Mikhail says through the phone. I'm sitting at the small table in the hotel room, flipping through the newspaper that was in front of my door this morning.

"What's taking so long anyway?" Mikhail asks.

"It's complicated," I tell him. I called Mikhail to ensure that no one was waiting on me to do a job back home. Mikhail is closest to Alek, so he'd know.

"Because she's a chick?" he asks.

"I don't know," I say honestly. I don't know what my hang-up is about with this woman. If she were a man, I would have killed her days ago. This is probably my body's way of reminding me that I still have a conscience even after all the shit that I've done.

"Well, don't take too long. Alek's patience is running thin, and since the whole marriage thing is over, he'll be more focused on cleaning up loose ends."

I run a hand over my face. I'm happy that the Miami Brotherhood took out Ivan. The guy was a dick, and there was enough chaos in the brotherhood after that Alek hasn't had the time to think about me. But from what Mikhail's saying, the dust is settling. This means Alek will be looking for something else to be pissed off about; me.

"Yeah, yeah, I'm on it." I hang up the phone and toss it on the table. I look out the window to see that it's gotten darker outside. I change into a pair of jeans and a nice shirt before grabbing my keys and heading out. I always get to the club early and linger in the parking lot. If Carmen doesn't show up, then I go back to the hotel. If she does show up, I ask for my dance and make sure she doesn't dance for any of these other assholes. It's selfish of me to ask for the dance. I could easily give her the money and tell her not to come back. But there are two things wrong with that.

One, Carmen doesn't seem to be the kind of woman to listen to anything someone else tells her to do, and two, The Motown gang already hates us, so leaving them short a stripper is just stirring the pot. To say they don't like me hanging around at their establishment is an understatement. They keep their eyes trained on me the entire time I'm here. The only reason they are participating in this little cat and mouse game I'm playing with Carmen is to keep a sliver of peace between the organizations. They're already on thin ice with the brotherhood since the Maven incident, and they know that a war with us would not end well. I'm not sure if Ruthless cares either way. He's quiet and likes to plan things ahead of time. So every day that I'm here is like a ticking time bomb as Ruthless finds out how to get rid of me without a war.

A flash of dark hair catches my eye, and I watch as Carmen walks across the parking lot. Her curvy body is covered in baggy sweatpants and a loose t-shirt. She's wearing chunky snow boots and a puffy coat over top of everything. She disappears inside, and I realize she never looks happy to be there. She's always sulking. I wait ten minutes past opening time before going inside. Joey gives me a dirty look as I walk past him but doesn't say anything. I let the bouncer know that I'm here for Carmen, and he leads me to the private room to wait. A few minutes later, she walks inside, transformed into a seductress. No matter how many times I've seen her like this, I can't get used to her beauty. Her curves, smooth skin, heart-shaped face with pouty lips, and wide eyes, she is every man's wet dream, but today she frowns at me. It's not her usual annoyance but something else.

"What's wrong?" I ask, sitting up on the dirty couch.

She closes the door and presses a button on the CD player. "Nothing. You wanted a dance. I'm giving you your dance."

She reaches out to dim the lights, but I beat her to the switch. She pinches her face up like she's tasted something sour.

"Can you move? I'm just trying to do my dance and go home."

I lean against the wall. "What's wrong?"

"I don't share my problems with customers."

I huff a laugh before reaching in my pocket and pulling out a couple of bills. This woman is costing me a shit-ton of money. I wave it in front of her face, and she reaches out to grab it, but I pull it away before she can.

"Tell me what's bothering you first."

She raises an eyebrow. "You're serious? You're giving me money to hear about my problems?"

I don't answer. With a sigh, she plops down in an empty chair. I sit back down on the couch. Every time I leave this place, I have to shower in scalding hot water. I hate to think that Carmen has to spend night after night here.

She runs a hand through her hair. "I'm just frustrated with everything. I'm fucking tired of Detroit. There's nothing here for us anymore. This city is dead and full of criminals. I don't want to be here every night, and I tried to talk to my sister, and it's like she's content with being stuck here. I'm not even thirty, and I feel like I'm at a dead-end."

I can hear the desperation in her voice. There's nothing worse than the feeling of being stuck. I'm not used to women coming out and expressing their feelings to me, so I'm not sure what to say. So I say the only thing I can think of.

"Did you eat?" I ask.

She looks at me, confused. "What?"

"Did you eat today?"

She shakes her head. "Not really. What does that have to do with anything?"

I stand to my feet. "Come on, let's go get some food."

She smiles. It's the first genuine smile I've seen out of her. It fits her face well.

"I have to work," she says, tugging the bottom corner of her lip into her mouth.

"Carmen," I say deeply. "Grab your stuff and meet me out in the parking lot."

"How do I know you aren't trying to kill me?"

That's what I should be doing. That's the whole reason I'm here in the first place, but I know I can't do it. I've tried to convince myself that I can, but I know the truth now.

"I'll be outside," is all I say before leaving the club. I wait in the parking lot, leaning against my jeep with my hands in my pocket. It's cold as balls in Detroit but not much worse than Boston.

I see her walk out of a side door dressed in the baggy clothes she came in with. She searches the small parking lot until her eyes land on me. She pulls her bottom lip into her mouth again before coming towards me. I walk around the jeep and open the door for her. Without a word, she jumps inside. If I were going to kill her, it would be so easy to do it right now.

"Where are we going?" she asks once I'm in the jeep.

"You tell me. I'm guessing you know what's open at this time."

I glance at the clock on the dashboard and realize it's only nine o'clock.

"Let's go to the pancake place. They're open all night. Sometimes the girls and I go after our shift. Take a right out of here."

She gives me directions to a small ranch-style building that's within walking distance to the club.

We go inside and get seated at a table close to the window. It's busier than I thought it would be, considering the time.

"The city wakes up at night," Carmen says, reading my facial expression.

"Why is that?" I ask.

She picks up the menu in front of her and spreads it open. "Because the jobs around here are limited. A lot of people turn to hustles that take place at night. Drugs, prostitution," she waves a hand over her body. "stripping. My sister is one of the lucky ones. She found something right outside the city."

"You live with her?"

She looks at me skeptically like she's not sure how much information to share.

"I've told you everything you wanted to know about me," I say.

The waitress comes up to our table. Carmen orders a coffee and a breakfast platter. I order the same since I haven't been paying attention to the menu. When the waitress disappears again, Carmen focuses back on me. Her eyes roam over my body, and I wonder what she's thinking. Is she attracted to me, or does she see a criminal who keeps throwing money at her to dance?

"She lives with me. Or I guess technically I live with her," she finally answers.

"Parents?"

"Gone." She doesn't elaborate.

I nod. "Mine too, murdered."

I don't know why I share that information. Maybe it's because I've become numb to the tragedy that happened to my parents. I've blocked out the dark months that followed after I came home to find them murdered in a puddle of blood. They went easy on my mom, shot her point-blank. I was thankful for that. But my dad wasn't so lucky.

"I'm sorry for your loss," she says quietly.

I shrug. "It's a risk you take when you join the Bratva."

"And you still joined?" she asked.

"I was furious after their murder, and joining the Bratva was the perfect way to get that anger out."

Her face changes, but I can't read her expression. "So I'm guessing you don't just sell drugs?"

"Would you feel better if I said yes?"

She nods. "I've dated drug dealers before."

"Hmm." I don't like the thought of her dating anyone, much less the street thugs around here.

The waitress chooses that moment to come back with our order. I sip my coffee while Carmen eats her food. She's purposely not making eye contact with me.

"You have the whole night off. So what's after this?"

She shrugs. "I guess go home."

I shake my head. "Maybe that's your problem."

"Excuse me."

"You need to have some fun. When's the last time you had any fun?"

She pops a piece of bacon in her mouth and chews while she thinks.

My lip twitches. "That means it's been too long. Let's go somewhere."

"Where?"

"You tell me."

Xavier

An hour later, I'm leaning against the bar at a nightclub, watching as Carmen dances. She's not dancing like in the strip club. She's enjoying it. She holds her drink up high in the air, so it doesn't spill as she moves her body to the beat. I take a sip of the cheap Whiskey as I watch her. Seeing her have fun like this makes me want to take her to the Bratva club and see how much fun she'd have there. The song ends, and she stops dancing to talk animatedly to the women surrounding her. She's been dancing for a while, and I'm surprised I haven't had to swat off a guy. They're looking at her, their eyes roaming over her body, but no one tries to approach. It's odd, and I file it away in my brain for later. A couple of songs later and she plops down in the empty seat next to me—a few pieces of hair stick to her sweaty forehead.

"You look so serious," she says.

My lip twitches. "I can't dance as well as you do."

She laughs, and it sounds so freeing. I can tell it's been a long time since she's genuinely laughed. The bartender gets her another drink, and she gulps half of it down. I haven't been keeping track of her drinks, but I know she's been throwing them back fast.

"Where are we going next?" she asks me.

I shrug. "You tell me."

She switches her lips back and forth as if trying to decide. "Honestly? I'm getting kind of tired. You've gotten me used to getting off work early."

I smile. "I'll take you home."

I finish the rest of my drink. I've been sipping on this weak Whiskey since we got here, so I'm completely sober.

She runs a soft hand over my bicep. "I don't want to go home."

She looks up at me with those big, brown eyes that look innocent, but I know they're sinister.

I nod and take her hand, leading her through the crowd of people until we're outside. The cold air is a relief from the hot, crowded club. We get into my jeep, and I head towards my hotel just outside the city.

"Where are you staying?" she asks as we move further out of downtown.

"A hotel."

I won't elaborate because I don't know the area well enough to explain where it's at. We'll be there soon enough.

"Hmm, so how temporary is your stay in Detroit?"

"I came to do a job. Once it's done, I'll go back to Boston." I don't mention the fact that she's the job and I've already failed at it.

She raises an eyebrow. "Ok, I have to know. What do you do? Does it involve prostitution? Oh God, are you trying to traffic me?!"

I glance at her. "No... but you should think about that before you get in a stranger's car."

She crosses her arms over her chest. "Do you kill people?"

I don't reply, and the quietness between us stretches on. She seems to be absorbing this information as I pull into the hotel parking lot and put the jeep in park.

"Why?"

"In the Brotherhood, we all have jobs. Every job is important to keep the operation running. I happen to be good at killing people." I stare at her, trying to gauge her reaction.

"How many people?"

"Do you really want to know?"

She takes a second to think about it. "No, I don't."

I sigh. "I should take you home."

I reach for the keys, ready to start the jeep back up, but she puts her hand over mine.

"No. I'm having fun tonight, remember?"

I can't read this woman. I just told her that I kill people for a living, and she still wants to go up to my hotel with me. Maybe I'm the one that should be concerned about her.

I remove the key and get out. I led her into the hotel, through the lobby, and up to my suite on the top floor. I swipe the key card and wave her inside. She steps inside and looks around the space. There's nothing interesting about it, just a plain hotel room, but she seems to be in awe.

I clear my throat. "You can borrow some of my clothes if you want to change."

She snaps out of whatever trance she's in and faces me. "Yeah, that'd be great."

I walk across the same living area and into the bedroom. I ruffle through my suitcase and pull out a pair of sweatpants and a t-shirt. Then I turn to look over at her; she's leaning against the door frame. My clothes will swallow her. She must be thinking the same thing because she says, "I'll just take the shirt."

I nod and close up my suitcase before handing her the plain black t-shirt.

"You didn't drink much at the club," she says.

"I had to drive."

Her lips twist up. "You're very responsible for a murderer."

I laugh.

"Well, now that you don't have anywhere to go, you can drink, right? Maybe you need to have some fun tonight too," she tempts me.

The words weren't meant to be seductive, but they sound so dirty coming off her tongue.

"I guess so," I reply.

She walks to the mini-fridge and pulls out two small bottles of alcohol. She tosses one to me, and I catch it. We both unscrew the top.

She raises her bottle in the air. "To a night of fun."

I raise mine in acknowledgment, and we both down it.

Carmen

A vibrating sound flutters into my dreams. I squeeze my eyes shut, hoping that the noise goes away. It does, but then it starts right back up again. Even behind my closed eyes, I can feel my head pounding. I feel slightly dizzy, like if I sit up right now, I might throw up. With my eyes still shut, I reach a hand out and feel around the blankets until I come across the rectangle device. I crack one eye open just enough to see the screen and press the green button.

"Hello," I croak. My throat feels dry and brittle.

"Are you ok?!" My sister screeches, her panic coming through the phone.

"Yeah."

"You asshole. I've been so fucking worried about you. When you weren't here when I woke up, I waited around, figuring you just had a late night, but then I started to get really scared. Where the hell are you, and why didn't you call me?"

Her words fly at me so fast it takes several seconds for me to comprehend what she's asking. Where am I? I slowly open my eyes all the way, relieved to see that the room is still dark due to thick curtains covering the windows. I look around the hotel room, and some of the memories of last night start to come back to me. Someone snores and the sound damn near makes me jump out of my skin.

"Shit!" I yelp.

"Carmen? What's wrong?"

I turn to see Xavier peek an eye open at me. He's sprawled out on the other side of the bed. His shirt is off and maybe his pants too, but I can't see because half of his body is covered up by the comforter. He's laying on his stomach, his perfectly sculpted face facing me. The grooves between his back muscles are incredibly deep, like each one has been conditioned individually to build this massive man.

"Carmen!" my sister shouts, turning my attention back to the phone.

"I'm ok, sorry, I'm safe. I'll be home soon."

I hang up before she can ask more questions that I don't feel like answering, especially in front of Xavier. He's staring at me with a slightly red eye.

"What did you do to me?" he asks, his voice deep and husky. I run a hand over my face, trying to clear my brain. I remember coming back here with him and drinking, but I don't remember much after that. I slowly pull myself into a sitting position, hoping to stop my head from spinning. I look around the hotel room. The pillows from the couch are on the floor, the tv stand, with the tv on it, has been moved in front of the bedroom door. I guess in our drunken state, we decided we needed to watch the tv right at the end of the bed. For the first time since waking up, I look down at what I'm wearing: an oversized t-shirt and my underwear. I'm not sure what to make of that. Xavier flips over to his back and puts his hands behind his head. His muscles ripple with the movement, and even in my confused hungover state, I can't help being mesmerized by him. God, he's a beautiful man.

"What...what happened last night?" I ask, embarrassed by the fact that I can't remember anything.

He raises an eyebrow. "You don't remember?"

I shake my head, which is a mistake because my brain screams in protest.

"We drank, you got very drunk, we talked, you...rearranged, and then we passed out."

"So we didn't...." I trail off, not wanting to say the words. If I did sleep with Xavier in my drunken state, I can't say I would regret it.

"No."

He sits up on the side of the bed and pulls his sweatpants on over his boxers.

"Hungover?" he asks me.

"Fuck yeah, aren't you?"

He chuckles. "I'm a big man. It's going to take a lot more than that to knock me out. I'll get you some pickle juice."

"Pickle juice?"

He walks to his suitcase and pulls out a t-shirt. He throws it over his head, covering the body I've been ogling. "It will cure your hangover."

"I should probably go. My sister is freaking out because I didn't come home last night." I glance at the hotel alarm clock. It's nearly eight o'clock.

"I'll take you."

After changing back into the clothes I wore last night and gathering the little bit of stuff I'd taken into the room, we headed out to his Jeep. There's a tension between us as he drives. I'm not sure what to say. What happens after this? We had a fun night together, and I've established that he's not a weirdo.

He stops at a gas station and runs inside. He comes back minutes later with a jar of pickles in his hand and a bottle of water. Thank God, my throat feels like it's on fire.

"Here. Drink the juice when you get home. It will help."

"Thank you," I say before taking both items. I immediately take the top off the water bottle and guzzle it. When he pulls on to my street, I look over at him.

"How do you know where I live?" I ask.

"Do you work tonight?" he asks, completely ignoring my question.

I shake my head, obviously not learning my lesson from earlier as it starts to pound again.

"Come out with me," he says, pulling over in front of the duplex.

I let out a short laugh. "Oh no, I'm not drinking that much two nights in a row."

His lip twitches. "Not drinking. We'll get dinner."

Butterflies fill my stomach. Is this his way of asking me on an actual date? I've never been out on a real date before. All the guys I've dated in the past were friends first, and it naturally progressed into a relationship. If I had any doubts about Xavier's intentions, they're clear now. He wants me.

"How long before you have to go back to Boston?" I ask. There's no point in me getting too involved if he's just going to leave soon.

"Let me worry about that."

I hesitate, not sure if this is something I really want to pursue. There's no question that Xavier is hot as sin, and I enjoyed his company last night, but this date seems serious.

He brings his face close to mine, and my breath hitches for a second. He smells like pine and fresh mint. "Listen, don't overthink it. It's just dinner."

Letting out a sigh, I nod. "Ok."

My eyes are glued to his lips, and neither of us seems to be breathing. He grabs the bottom of my chin between two of his large fingers and tilts my head up. He presses his lips to mine, and my body melts at the contact. Our lips fit together perfectly, and the kiss is so smooth like we've done it a thousand times. He doesn't turn it into anything more, doesn't try to take control of my mouth, or demand entrance. It's a surprisingly soft kiss for such a dangerous man. He pulls back and lets my chin go. His eyes have darkened with desire, and something sparks deep in my belly as his tongue jets out to lick at his bottom lip as if getting one more taste.

"I'll pick you up at seven."

I nod like a bobblehead because I'm suddenly dizzy again, and this time it's not because of the hangover. I climb out of the Jeep and walk into the house with pickle juice and water in hand.

Carmen

The front door closing wakes me from my nap. I've been recovering from my hangover all day. I was relieved when I got home to see that Sierra had left me a note on the kitchen table. She was running errands, but we would 'talk' when she got back. I check my phone, and it's past five o'clock now. I hear her footsteps in the hallway a second before she jiggles the handle of my locked bedroom door.

"Carmen," she scolds like an angry mother. I drag myself out of bed and unlock the door. She steps inside as I sit back down on the mattress.

She flips on the overhead light, and I have to shield my eyes from the sudden intrusion of light.

She throws her hands in the air. "What happened?"

"If you sit down, I'll tell you. Calm down."

She looked around the room before perching her ass on the office chair.

"It was that guy wasn't it? The one who's been giving you all the money?"

I hate how she says it like that. It makes me feel dirty.

"Yeah, I was having a bad day when I got to the club, so he took me out to get some food, and then we had some drinks."

She raises an eyebrow. "And where did you sleep?"

I swallow. "His hotel room."

"Hotel room?!"

"We didn't do anything," I say before she can jump to the conclusion. "We just hung out and had fun."

She runs a hand over her face in frustration. "Carmen, what are you doing with this guy?"

I shrug. "I don't know. He's taking me on a date tonight."

"And why is he staying in a hotel room?"

"He's from Boston. He's here on business," I say, not wanting to tell Sierra what kind of business that is. She's already disappointed enough.

"Carmen, if you think this guy is your ticket out of here-"

"I don't. I like him."

She looks surprised. "You do?"

"Yeah, he's...I don't know. Better than any of the guys around here. He's scary looking, big as hell, but he saw I was upset last night, and he made my night better than I could have asked for. He's the first guy ever to ask me on a date."

Sierra looks sympathetic, like I'm some poor lost puppy.

"Don't give me that look," I snap.

"I'm not trying to, but I wouldn't be a good older sister if I weren't worried. If you're just having fun, then fine, but be careful. I don't want you to get hurt. Men are known to promise women the sun and the moon, then not deliver either one. I just don't want that to happen to you."

I can't blame Sierra for being a skeptic. She's always had a big heart, and we're the only family we have left.

"I know. I love you. Don't worry about me. I'll be okay," I assure her.

She gives me a sad smile before standing to her feet.

"Alright," she says before leaving.

****

I'm just finishing up my make-up when there's a knock at the door. It feels good getting dressed up for something that's not a strip club. I'm not sure where we're going, so I choose a long sleeve dress with leggings underneath and a blazer over the top. It's casual enough, but it will also work if he takes me somewhere fancy. Sierra's footsteps sound on the floor a moment before I hear the door open.

"Oh...uh wow, you are big," I hear her say, and it takes everything in me to cover up my laugh. I stand up from the crossed-legged position where I've been sitting in front of my full-length mirror. Xavier says something back to her, but I can't make out the words. I straighten my clothes and pull on a pair of black booties before opening my bedroom door.

"And is that where you work?" I hear my sister ask as I come around the corner to the kitchen. Xavier is standing near the table with his hands tucked in the pockets of his slacks. He looks good tonight. The button-down shirt he wears is loose, and he's rolled the sleeves up to show off his muscular and veiny arms. He didn't bother shaving, and I'm glad for that. I like his slightly rugged look. His eyes drift away from my sister to me. His eyes roam over me before the corner of his mouth twitches like he wants to smile.

"You look beautiful," he says, not giving a damn that my sister is right there and can hear him. I like that about Xavier. He's not embarrassed or scared of anyone. He speaks the truth, and whatever's on his mind, no matter the consequences.

I swallow. "Thanks."

Sierra looks back and forth between us. "Where are you guys going tonight?"

I roll my eyes at her. "I'll be fine, mom."

She flips me the bird, and I chuckle.

"You like seafood?" Xavier asks me.

"Love it."

He nods. "Good, I have a place in mind."

He opens the front door for me. I grab my coat off the hook next to the door and slip it on. I give my sister one last I'll be fine look before stepping out the door.

"It was nice to meet you, Sierra," Xavier says before joining me on the porch. We walked across the street to where he parked the Jeep. It's so shiny and new it looks out of place on my street.

Fifteen minutes later, we pulled up to a restaurant in downtown Detroit. It's in a plaza lined with home decor stores and upscale boutiques.

"I love this area," I say as Xavier parks the Jeep.

"Yeah?"

I nod. "It's so pretty here. It's strange to think how close it is to where I live. It's like two different worlds."

He gets out and comes around to open the door for me. He holds my hand as we walk into the restaurant. His hand is rough and calloused. I wonder if it's from the workouts he does. A man his size has to be lifting weights. The hostess greets us with a big smile and shows us to our table. It's in the back corner of the restaurant, so we're hidden by the shadows. I'm happy about that just in case someone recognizes me. Anyone who knows my brother would love to tell him about a date I went on. Not that I care what Ruthless thinks, but I have a feeling that would cause trouble for Xavier.

"You're nervous," Xavier says from across the table.

"A little bit."

He gets up from his side of the booth and slides in next to me. It's cheesy, but I do feel calmer with him sitting beside me. It makes the date seem more casual. I take off my coat and set it next to me on the booth.

A waitress comes over and gets our drink order. I order a strawberry lemonade while he gets water.

"You try to eat healthily?" I ask as I scan the menu.

"I try to. I work out a lot, so it's important that I don't waste my time in the gym by eating shit."

He's set his elbows on the table, and I notice how wide his arms are. Yeah, he definitely spends a lot of time in the gym.

"Dancing is my workout, but I still eat like shit."

He laughs. "You don't need to diet. You're perfect."

The waitress comes back with our drinks, and we place our food order. When she leaves again, I feel myself getting hot. Something about being this close to Xavier in the dark corner of the restaurant has me squeezing my thighs together. He notices because he grabs my thigh and squeezes. Damn, that feels good. I look up at him, but he's drinking his water like nothing is happening under the table.

"Your sister seems nice," he says. He turns to look at me with mischief in his dark eyes. So this is the game he wants to play.

"She's unsure about you."

His hand moves to my inner thigh, and my legs open on command. I'm already wet, and my nipples grow hard. Maybe I should be embarrassed, but I feel safe with Xavier even as he inches up my thigh towards my center.

"Why is that?" he asks.

I have to remember what we're talking about. Oh yeah, Sierra.

"She's just protective."

His hand rests right on my center, and I shift in the booth, trying to get some friction. My body is begging for him to move his hand, to rub me right there. I feel desperate, but I don't care.

"She's older than you?" he asks.

I look at him, and he's smiling at me. He knows exactly what he's doing.

"Yes," I say sharply.

As if satisfied with my answer, he rubs small circles over the fabric of my clothes. It's just enough to make me want him even more. I could really give a damn about this restaurant. I need this man between my legs and hovering over me. I'd be surprised if he didn't have a big dick considering all the big dick energy he seems to give off. He presses harder against my sex, and I bite my lips to keep from panting. My pussy tingles with every movement of his hand. I close my eyes briefly, and when I open them again, he's staring at me. He must like seeing the expression on my face as he pushes me towards the edge. But then he moves his hand away.

"What-"

Before I can ask, the waitress comes up to the table. I straighten in the booth, and heat comes to my cheeks.

"Here you go," she says while setting down our food. I was hungry for food when we got to the restaurant, but now I'm hungry for something else entirely.

"Eat up," he says. "We have a long night ahead of us."

Carmen

We eat fast, and when we get back to his hotel, we stand across from each other in the small kitchenette. The air shifts between us, and he pushes off the counter. He comes close to me until we're just an inch apart. His scent of pine and fresh mint fill my nose. I squeeze my thighs together as those dark eyes stare at me. Not at my body or my cleavage, just me. I have to crane my neck to look up at him, and his expression is full of lust, probably just like mine. He doesn't make a move, letting me decide what I want to do tonight.

"Xavier," I breathe.

He places his hands on the counter next to my ass and bends down to whisper in my ear. His breath tickles my neck.

"Yeah, baby?"

The way he calls me baby sends a zap to my core. My nipples grow hard against my bra.

"I want you," I admit.

I want him so fucking bad. I need to feel him between my legs, watching as his beautiful body hovers on top of me. After working in the strip club, I thought I'd become immune to the desire for sex. That's far from the truth. I just needed the right person to whisper in my ear. Xavier is that person. He bites down on my neck, causing me to arch my back.

Goosebumps rise over my skin. I slip my hands over his shirt and feel every hard muscle in his stomach. There's not one ounce of fat on this man. He's sculpted from marble. He grabs the back of my thighs and lifts me onto the counter. I instantly wrap my arms around his neck. My body temperature has risen like someone turned up the heat. I need him inside me like a fish needs water. I go for his jeans, but he stops me.

I look up at him.

"What?" I ask, slightly annoyed that he stopped me.

"You sure you want this? I'm not the kind of man to buy you flowers. I'm leaving Detroit-"

"I want you to fuck me," I say, cutting him off. I can care about all that shit later.

He smirks before grabbing me once again. I wrap my legs around him, and he walks us to the bed. He lays me down softly before standing up again.

"Clothes, off," he grunts out like a caveman. He watches with smoldering eyes as I strip off my clothes. I'm used to taking my clothes off for men, but it feels so much more intimate with Xavier in his hotel room. When I'm fully naked, I lay back on the bed with my hands above my head. I hear him suck in air before he grabs my legs and pulls me to the edge of the mattress. Before I know it, he's down on his knees with his face between my legs. I nearly jump off the bed in surprise, but he puts a hand on my stomach, holding me down as he licks a clean line through my folds.

"Oh shit," I moan as his mouth devours me. I grab his short hair, needing something to pull on as he makes my pussy his. There's no hesitation as he licks and sucks. He inserts two fingers inside me, and I struggle to keep my legs open as I climb closer to the edge. He uses his free hand to pin my leg to the bed, so I stay open for him. He doesn't acknowledge my shaky legs or my death grip on him. He keeps going like all his focus is on my pussy, and his concentration can't be broken. He's a starved man eating a steak. I've never had a man completely ravage me like this. There's something so primal about it.

"I'm about to come," I moan. In response, he sucks on my clit and increases the speed of his fingers fucking me. An electric shock runs through my body, and I'm hit with the most overwhelming orgasm I've ever had.

"Oh shit!" I cry out. My head becomes fuzzy like a static TV channel. My vision blurs as I start to come down. He slows his speed as my breathing returns to normal levels. He stands up, looking down at me. My legs feel heavy, my body is entirely spent. He wipes his mouth with the back of his hand before he takes off his clothes.

"We're far from done tonight, baby," he warns me. If I wasn't so high off my climax, I might have been scared. He strips off his boxers revealing the most giant dick I've ever seen. It's thick, veiny, and belongs to a man of Xavier's size. He palms his dick and slowly strokes it. I watch in awe, unsure of what's next. He looks to me and then to the floor in front of him. He doesn't need to say anything because, after the orgasm that he just gave me, I'm happy to return the favor. I kneel in front of him, the carpet digging into my knees. He grabs my chin, so I have to look up at him. I've never been a woman to submit to a man, but there's something about Xavier that has me breaking all my rules.

"I want it slow, everything slow," he says, his voice taking on a commanding tone. It reminds me of the first time I met him. I try to nod, but I can't with his fingers holding my chin. He lets me go, and I stare at his massive dick in front of me. I grip the base and lick the underside from the base to the tip. He lets out a groan that sends a zap to my core. I continue slowly licking all sides of him before finally taking him in my mouth. I take him as far down as I can, nearly getting to the base before I gag. He lets out another groan and wraps my hair in his hand. He guides my head to the pace he likes. I don't mind letting him take control. He seems to grow bigger in my mouth, and I glance up to see his heavy eyes are trained on me with a look of desire.

"Keep looking at me," he grunts while continuing to guide me up and down his cock. I do as he says, watching his facial expression change as pleasure takes over his features. When I think he's going to come, he pulls back.

"On the bed. I need to be inside that pussy."

I clench at his dirty words before standing to my feet and laying back on the bed.

"On all fours," he commands. He pulls me to the edge of the bed and lines his cock up with my entrance. I brace myself for his intrusion, but as he promised, he enters me slowly. I can feel every single inch of him as he spreads me. When I think he's all in, he keeps going. I grip the sheets as my body adjusts to him. I'm so full I'm worried he's not going to fit all the way. He plants a kiss on my exposed shoulder.

"Relax," he says. For such an intimidating man, he seems to enjoy taking his time when it comes to sex. I take a deep breath, relaxing my muscles as he pushes in the rest of the way. He reaches under me and rubs small circles around my still sensitive clit.

A moan escapes my lips.

"You're going to come all over my dick, baby." I'm not sure if that's a promise or a threat, but either way, my body seems to respond to his words. He continues rubbing me as he fucks me from behind. He speeds up his pace, hitting me just where I need him to.

"Oh shit."

"Say my name," he demands.

My legs shake as pleasure spreads through my body. Using his other hand, he slaps my ass, bringing my attention back to the present.

"Say my name," he repeats.

"Xavier!" The word leaves my lips just as the second orgasm overwhelms me. My walls pulsate around his dick, milking him. He speeds up to a merciless pace. I try to catch my breath, and then he lets out a noise that resembles a growl as he grips my hips and holds himself inside me. I can feel his dick throb before he fills me with cum. So much cum that when he pulls out, it leaks onto the sheets.

I roll over to my back, not able to hold myself up any longer. My body is weak, and my eyes flutter close.

Carmen

I'm not sure when it became a routine, but we quickly fell into it. I stopped going to the club altogether. There was no point in going when Xavier would just show up, throw money at me and somehow convince Joey to let me go home.

I started waking up at a regular time, writing in the morning, and spending my nights with Xavier in his hotel room. Sometimes we went out to get food or went to a bar, but most nights, we stayed in that room wrapped around each other. I never asked him what he did during the day, and we didn't talk about when he was leaving. At some point, he's going to go back to Boston, and I'll have to go back to the club, but I don't want to think about that. I want to enjoy this moment while it's here.

I walk into the club at two o'clock. I need to grab a couple of things from my locker. When I walk in, I'm surprised to see that Ruthless's office door is wide open. I peek my head inside to see him leaning back in the chair and rolling a blunt between his fingers. I should leave before he notices me.

"Come in, Carmen," he says, the annoyance evident in his tone.

I roll my eyes before walking into his office. It smells like weed and cheap perfume, probably from a woman that recently left.

"I'm just grabbing a couple of things," I say, sinking into the chair across from him.

"Justin says you haven't been around the club lately."

I don't respond. I don't owe Ruthless anything, not even an explanation for my absence.

"Xavier Kane is not a good man, Carmen," he says, putting down the blunt and finally looking at me dead on.

I hold back a scoff. "I'm aware. Thanks for your input on my dating life, Trey."

Using his real name always pisses him off. He has no right to pass judgment considering all the shit the Motown gang does under his rule.

His jaw twitched, the only indication I get that I've gotten under his skin.

"Dating, huh? He's going back to Boston soon because if he doesn't, we'll make sure he does. I've been civil, haven't I? I'm trying to avoid a war on our turf, but your new fuck buddy is out staying his welcome."

"We're not fuck buddies," I snap, immediately regretting my words because if we're not fuck buddies, then what are we?

Ruthless smirks, and it's one of those deadly smirks that look more sinister than amused. "He's the hitman for the Russian mafia. Have you asked him why he's here? Why do you think a killer from Boston would come to Detroit, little sister? I know you didn't finish college, but you're smarter than that."

His insult stings, but I don't let him see just how much. I don't say anything because I know my brother better than almost anyone, and he's pissed. When he's pissed...he snaps. I have no desire to be at the receiving end of that.

He lets out a frustrated breath and leans back in his chair. "You're a witness. The Russian's don't leave witnesses."

It takes a minute for his words to digest. Xavier is a hitman. I'm a witness. I stand up from the chair so fast it topples over.

I don't bother picking it up before storming out of the club. I don't even bother grabbing my shit from the locker because it looks like I'll be coming back here. Just where Ruthless wants me.

Xavier

The bouncer standing guard outside the club puts his hand on my chest as I try to walk inside. I push his hand off and crowd him against the wall so fast he's not even aware of what just happened.

"Don't fucking touch me," I growl. Usually, I'm better at keeping my temper in check, but I've been trying to get a hold of Carmen for the last two days, and she's gone completely radio silent. One day we were rolling around in my sheets, and the next day she disappeared.

"You've outstayed your welcome," a voice says from behind me. I let the bouncer go and turn to see Justin standing in the doorway.

"I'm just here to get Carmen."

"I'm not talking about the club; I'm talking about the city. You've had enough time to complete whatever business you needed to get done here. We've been generous, but now it's gone on too long. I suggest you leave tonight."

Three more men come to the door to back Justin up. Fuck, I hadn't planned on this. If Alek weren't already pissed at me, he would be now that I've managed to piss off the Motown gang.

"Is Carmen here?" I ask.

He laughs. "You're one stupid-"

"I'd be careful if I were you." I don't give a damn how many men are in there. I'll take them out myself before I let someone insult me.

Justin narrows his eyes. I turn around and walk away. It might be stupid for me to turn my back on them, but I'm not afraid of any fucking body.

"She's not here, but if I were you, I'd be really careful about fucking around with Ruthless's sister."

I freeze. Sister?

"Looks like you two have a lot to talk about."

I hear the big, heavy door shut behind me.

*****

I ball my hand into a fist and pound on the door again. "I'm not going away."

To my surprise the door is swung open, and Carmen's sister, Sierra, stands there in pajama pants and an oversized shirt with a cat on it.

"Will you knock it off? She doesn't want to talk to you, and unlike you crazy people I have-"

I push past her, not in the mood to be a gentleman. Carmen will find out soon enough that I'm not a gentleman anyway, so why not now.

"Hey!" Sierra shouts from behind me. I walk down the hallway of the small duplex. Opening the first door, I realize it's a bathroom. The second door opens up to a nicely decorated but messy bedroom. Carmen jumps up from where she's sitting, crossed-legged on the bed. An open journal and pen lay forgotten on the mattress. She's dressed in shorts, so goddamn short, they might as well be underwear. Her thick thighs are on full display, and my dick instantly hardens. No matter how annoyed I am with this woman, she can always get me hard.

"What-"

I close the door. "We need to talk."

When I turn back around, her eyes are wide with fear. It reminds me of the night I took Maven. She'd been terrified.

"So you're scared of me now?" I ask.

She crosses her arms over her chest, and I don't miss the way it pushes her tit to the top of her thin tank top.

"You lied to me," she says.

I tilt my head to the side, trying to figure out what the hell she's talking about. I've been candid with this woman. I told her about the brotherhood, about my parents, everything except for why I came here in the first place. Shit.

"Who told you?"

She takes a step away from me, towards the bed, and that's when I see it. The butt of a handgun sticks out from under her pillowcase. She notices the moment I realize her intention, and we both go for the gun. She reaches it before I do and aims it at me. She holds it out away from her body like she's scared of the kickback.

"Have you used a gun before?" I ask.

Her eyes are wild, but not wild enough for me to believe she'll pull the trigger. "Don't test me," she grits out.

I take a step closer to her, and she cocks the gun.

"I'm serious, Xavier. You need to start talking."

"Baby, we're not talking about anything until you get that gun out of my face."

She tightens her grip, which only manages to piss me off. There's a knock on her bedroom door, and it's enough of a distraction that I grab her wrist, squeezing right at the pressure point, so she has no option but to drop the gun. I catch it in my other hand before wrestling her to the ground. She slaps and yells, trying to escape as if I'm the one who just held her at gunpoint.

The bedroom door handle jiggles, and Sierra is now banging on the door. "Carmen!Carmen!"

I manage to keep her body pinned under mine as I unload the gun and toss it across the room. Carmen gives up her fight, realizing that I'm ten times her size and she's wasting energy.

"Do you honestly think if I were going to kill you, I'd take you out to dinner first? You think that I'd invite you to my hotel, take you out to bars," I lower my voice and whisper in her ear. "Do you think I'd fuck you?"

Those big brown eyes look up at me. She's lost some of the fight, but I can still see the unease.

"Talk to me, Baby," I plead. "I'll tell you whatever you want to know."

"I'm calling the cops!" Sierra yells. I've managed to pretty much tune her out, but that gets my attention. I look at Carmen, pleading with her to listen to me. She rolls her eyes.

"Don't, Sierra! I'm fine," she shouts.

The doorknob rattles again. "Open the door if you're fine."

I give her one last look before letting her go. We both stand to our feet. She smooths down her hair and straightens her clothes before opening the door. Sierra storms into the room, looking around for any signs of danger. If she sees the gun on the floor, she doesn't comment. She looks between the two of us.

"I don't know what kind of freaky shit you two are into, but I have work in the morning."

If the situation wasn't so serious, I might laugh at that. Sierra storms back out and slams the door. Carmen and I stare at each other. She looks hot as hell when she's flustered like this. Her cheeks are slightly pink from our tussle, and her hair is still wild despite her small effort to smooth it down. Her nipples poke through her tank top.

"Did you come to Boston to kill me?" she asks, point-blank. I notice she stays close to the door, probably in case she needs to run. I stuff my hands in my pockets.

"Yes, that was the plan."

Her eyes widened. She expected me to deny it.

"Why am I still standing in this room with you?" she mumbles to herself.

"Because you know I'm not going to hurt you. I might be a murderer, but I'm not into torture. I don't play with my food. I go in, get the job done, and come back home."

"Then what makes me so different?" she asks. It's the same question I've been asking myself since I got that first dance from her.

"I've never been assigned to kill a woman, an innocent."

She scoffs, and I take a step closer to her so she'll listen to me. I need her to hear me when I say what's next.

"I kill bad men, Carmen. Men that have done things far worse than what I've ever done. I don't feel remorse when I kill them. Sometimes I feel some sick relief like I'm ridding the world of these assholes. But you're not that. You're the most beautiful woman I've ever met. You're strong, fierce, and everything that the world needs more of. I couldn't hurt you if I tried. I'm putting everything at risk by still being here. I have an allegiance to my brotherhood. I follow orders without asking questions. Alek could easily kill me for going against a direct order. But I'm okay with that because I'll risk my life for yours any day."

She's quiet, but I can see that my words must have gotten through to her because she relaxes her defensive stance.

"Let me touch you, Baby," I plead. Who knew a couple of days would turn me into such a pussy. She gives a slight nod, so I wrap her in my arms. I'm surprised when she wraps her arms around my waist and buries her face in my shirt. She shudders. All the adrenaline is leaving her body. Wetness seeps through my shirt. I kiss the top of her head.

"Are you crying?" I ask.

"No."

I smile at her stubbornness. We stayed there for a long while, both of us trying to digest what just happened. I have no idea what I'm doing with Carmen, but I know I can't leave Detroit without her. She finally pulls away and looks up at me, her eyes slightly red.

"I'm sorry. I should have told you-"I start.

"You should have. Don't lie to me again about anything," she demands.

I want to ask her about Ruthless and how she failed to mention that he's her brother but now is not the time.

"I promise," I vow before taking her chin in my fingers and tilting her head back. I press my lips to hers. They're soft and puffy from crying. She wraps her arms around my shoulders, standing on her tiptoes to reach me. Her petite body presses against my hard one. We fit together perfectly. She's everything I'm not, spontaneous, messy, stubborn, but most of all, she's soft. I'm a boulder, and she's a blanket. My dick hardens as we continue to kiss. I grab her hips, digging my fingers into her bare skin.

"Bed," I grunt out.

Xavier

It's been two days since I've been between her legs, and I was having withdrawals. We don't break our kiss as I walk us to her small bed. I lay her down on the mattress, pushing away papers to make room. I fit perfectly in between her thighs. Breaking our kiss, I suck on her neck. Her sweet scent hits me in the face. It's the same scent that has lingered on my pillows. I refused to let the housekeepers clean in case they washed out her smell. Her back arched as I trailed kisses down to her cleavage.

"Xavier," she moans.

I stop to press a finger to her lips. I don't know how close her sister's bedroom is to this one, but I don't want any interruptions. She nods understanding without me having to say anything. Her perfectly round tits stare back at me after I lift her tank top over her head. I flick my tongue over her brown nipple, which causes her to grab my bicep, squeezing tightly. This woman is fucking perfection. I tease her nipples, pulling them into my mouth one at a time until her nails are digging into my skin.

"I can make you come just from this," I say.

Her eyes plead with me.

"But I won't."

"Xavier," she moans, already out of breath.

I ignore her and continue my descent. I pull off her pajama shorts, relieved to see that there's nothing underneath. Her smooth, bare pussy greets me. I lick my thumb before rubbing it between her folds. Her body lights up.

She grabs her breasts, rubbing her tits as I play with her clit. I love how responsive she is. She doesn't just lay there and let me do all the work. She's eager to reach her orgasm and get me to mine.

"Keep going, baby," I command, loving the way she touches herself. Her eyes pop open as if she forgot I was in the room. My lip twitches in amusement. She continues rubbing herself as I insert two fingers inside her. She's so fucking tight around my fingers. She gasps at the intrusion, and her breathing starts to pick up. Right when she's about to fall over the edge, I pull away. Her eyes pop open again, this time with annoyance. But that look doesn't last long as I quickly pull down my pants just enough to take out my dick and bury myself inside her.

"Oh shit," she moans before biting down on her lip as if remembering to stay quiet. Her tight pussy might be the closest I'll ever get to heaven.

"Fuck, Baby, you're so damn tight." Her walls squeeze my dick like a viper, and she's not even trying. I want to fuck her hard; since I'm still angry because she didn't tell me about Ruthless, because she aimed a gun at me, because she's mine. I hike both her legs over my shoulder, so she's forced to keep them open as I pound into her. The bed creaks loudly underneath us. Her nails dig into my back so hard she might draw blood.

"Oh shit," she says breathlessly, a mix of surprise and pleasure in her tone. Up until this point, I've fucked her the way I've wanted to. Now I'm fucking her the way I need to.

"Come for me," I whisper as I slam into her, over and over again. She's almost there. I can hear it in her breathing.

"I...I.." she stops talking, and I watch as her orgasm hits her. I clamp my hand over her mouth as she lets out a sound between a moan and a scream. But I don't slow down my pace. Our sweat mixes together as I continue to punish her pussy. She pushes on my chest. The stimulation is becoming too much for her. She lets out a string of curses.

"I'm not done," I grunt out even as my dick grows harder, and I start to feel my balls tighten.

"It's too much," she begs because she's never been fucked like this, I'm sure of it. Now that she's come, her body is sensitive. But just as my balls tighten even more and I bury myself inside her. Her legs start to shake, and she comes again. I empty myself inside of her as her walls milk my cock for all it has.

Carmen

"So that was crazy," Sierra says as I step out of my bedroom. I should have hid in my room until she left because this isn't a conversation I want to have. I use the hair tie on my wrist to tie my hair up in something that resembles a bun. Walking down the hall, I join her in the kitchen, where she sits down at the table and opens a book. She's already dressed for work; it looks like she's just waiting to leave.

"Sorry," I mumble, not sure what else to say. Xavier ended up leaving last night, saying he had some business he needed to take care of. As always, I didn't ask questions, but maybe I should start to.

"What's going on with you? You stopped working at the club, and now you're all wrapped up around this guy who is leaving town."

"I don't know," I admit.

Xavier has taken my heart, and he's not letting it go. Since he's given me so much money, I've been able to get caught up with all of our incoming bills. It's the first time in my life I've had the time to pursue things that I want to, specifically writing. I feel like I'm getting somewhere with the book I've been working on for years.

Sierra doesn't say anything else, probably picking up on the fact that she's not going to get answers. I can't give answers that I don't know myself.

After she leaves, I brew some coffee and sit down at the kitchen table with my notebook. This is the second notebook I've gone through, and my hands are starting to cramp from all the writing. I need to get a computer. Maybe if I start to save up, I can get a cheap one. I don't need anything fancy, just something to type on—an hour or so into writing, my phone buzzes.

Jessica's name flashes across the screen.

"Hey," I answer.

"Hey, girl, where have you been?" she asks.

"At home. I'm just taking...a sabbatical."

"Sabbatical? Fuck I need a sabbatical too," she says.

I laugh.

"Do you want to hang out today? I miss seeing you at the club. I have to deal with Justin bitching all damn night."

I glance over at the clock. It's getting close to lunchtime. "Sure, you wanna get some food?"

"Yeah, where at?"

"Pancake Place?" I suggest.

"Sounds good. I'll see you soon?"

"Yep."

We hang up, and I jump in the shower before changing into a pair of jeans and a long sleeve v-neck shirt. I'm too lazy to do my hair, so I try to smooth out the bun. I definitely look like a writer. The walk to Pancake Place is a short one, but she might beat me there since Jessica has a car. The small restaurant is pretty much empty since it's a weird time between breakfast and lunch. The hostess tells me to sit wherever I like. I do, taking a booth in the middle. It's not long before Jessica strolls inside. She's dressed in tight jeans, an oversized sweater, and heels. Her make-up looks fresh too. She spots me and immediately slides into the booth opposite of me. That's when I noticed my small duffle bag over her shoulder.

I raise an eyebrow.

"Ruthless wanted me to bring you this."

I roll my eyes. "Of course, he did."

Ruthless was pissed at me for reasons I still didn't understand. I take the bag from her, stuffing it in my corner of the booth.

The waitress comes to our table, and we order without needing a menu since this place is a staple for us.

"So what's going on? A sabbatical?" Jessica asks as soon as the waitress leaves.

I take a sip of my water.

"Rumors are circling the club," she says.

"What kind of rumors?"

"You know stupid shit, like that you quit because you got tired of Ruthless's bullshit."

I laugh. "That one isn't very far-fetched."

"Amber thinks you got pregnant."

I keep my smile in place as I think about that. When was my last period? I rake my brain; I've been seeing Xavier for at least a month, so it must be coming soon. I make a mental note to pick up some tampons on the way home.

The waitress comes back with our food, and Jessica fills me in on all the drama at the club. I listen, chiming in as needed. It's nice to talk to someone that's not my sister. I love my sister but hearing her lecture me is getting old.

"Hey, shouldn't you be asleep?" I ask as we stand to our feet to leave.

"Yeah, I should, but I'm off tonight, so I'm not worried about it."

We say our goodbyes and go our separate ways. I stop at the gas station on my way back and grab a pack of tampons. As I do the pregnancy test next to it catches my eye. Why the hell do they put pregnancy tests next to tampons anyway? It doesn't make sense. Something compels me to grab the box for the pregnancy test. It's silly, but why the hell not? I can't be pregnant. There's no way. I check out and walk back to the house. Once I set my stuff down, I stare at the pregnancy test peeking out from the gas station bag. If I'm going to keep staring at it, I might as well take the damn test. My mind made up, I snatch the box and go into the bathroom. I pee on the stick and set it on the counter to wait. When it's finally time to look down at the stick, my heart drops to my stomach.

Xavier

I check my phone surprised to see there's still nothing from Alek. I know he's busy, but he's been consistently blowing up my phone since I damn near landed in Detroit. Something doesn't feel right. There's a knock on the hotel door. I tuck my gun into my waist before going to answer it. I look through the peephole, surprised to see Carmen standing on the other side. I open the door, and she smiles at me, but I know something is wrong. She's dressed in one of those oversized puffy coats and a pair of tight jeans. As she brushes past me to walk inside, I can see that the jeans make her ass look amazing.

"What's going on? I was going to pick you up." I always pick her up.

"I decided just to get a cab." She sets her purse before sitting on the couch. I shut the door and turn to face her.

"Carmen, what the fuck is going on?"

Last night I thought something had changed between us, but maybe I was wrong.

"Can we relax? I don't want to talk right now," she pleads.

This is why I've never been a man to do relationships; women are complicated. I lean against the wall and watch as she grabs the remote and turns on the tv. She doesn't even watch tv.

"You know, I thought you were a more honest person," I say, knowing damn well it will piss her off.

"What is that supposed to mean?"

I shrug. "You know, you just seemed like someone who wouldn't hide shit from me. Guess I was wrong."

"Me? Hiding something from you? That's rich. Fuck you-"

A loud crack comes from the door followed by two bangs so loud my brain doesn't comprehend what's happening. I pull out my gun and have it cocked and pointing towards the door as Alek kicks it down. I've seen Alek kill plenty of men and the look on his face is the same now as it was when he killed them. He's shut off his emotions, like it's a switch, so he can get the job done. I know because I do it too.

Carmen screams.

"Sorry to break up this little party," Alek says like he's not the least bit bothered by kicking down my hotel door. The other guests have probably already called the cops. I set my gun down on the table because killing Alek would be suicide. Even if I manage to kill him, the rest of the brotherhood will hunt me down.

I turn to see Carmen standing on her feet, looking back and forth between us. The fear on her face is apparent, and she takes a couple of steps back, but the only way to get out is through the front door.

"No, stay," Alek barks.

"Fuck no," Carmen says, grabbing her bag from the floor. If I weren't so worried about her safety, I'd be amused. No one stood up to Alek.

Alek raises an eyebrow at her. "Then I'll make this quick."

He pulls his gun from his holster and points it at my forehead. I knew this was coming. He told me if I didn't kill her that he'd kill me, but for some reason, I'm still surprised. I regret nothing. As long as Carmen makes it out of here alive, it will be worth it.

"Stop! Wait, don't-" Carmen's words are cut off with a loud sob. The sound nearly breaks my heart in two.

"You had one fucking job, Xavier, kill her and come back to Boston, but instead, you stayed and fucked the target."

I look him in the eye. I'll never back down from any man, even with a gun pointed at my head.

"Don't hurt her," I say.

"That's what you're concerned about? How can you protect her when you're dead?"

"Please stop. I'll give you whatever you want," Carmen sobs.

"I want you dead," Alek says, his eyes flickering to her. Carmen looks at me. I'm the man that's supposed to protect her, but the only way I can at this moment is to get Alek to agree not to kill her. I know he'll kill me. I've accepted it, but my death will be in vain if she dies too.

"Do what you have to do, Alek but leave her out of it. I'm the one that went against orders. The way you feel about Delaney..."

His hand tightens on the gun. "Don't you dare compare my wife to this whore."

He cocks the gun, and I close my eyes. Alek won't kill her.

"Xavier! Stop! I'm pregnant!" Carmen shouts. My body goes stiff. I open my eyes and see tears streaming down her face. Alek looks just as shocked, and his arm loosened its hold on the gun.

Something in me snaps, and I take advantage of the distraction. I push the gun away from my face. It clatters to the floor, and Alek and I both stare at it.

He rubs a hand over his jaw and lets out a humorless laugh. "That's fucking great."

He looks torn. Alek might be merciless, but everyone has their weak spots. Sirens wail in the distance.

"Time is up. I'll make this right," I say to Alek.

"You both are coming to Boston tonight," Alek states. I know what's waiting for me in Boston because if Alek isn't going to kill me because I have a kid on the way, he'll at least make me suffer.

"Tonight," I agree. He takes one last look at Carmen before leaving.

Carmen

I can't breathe. My chest is moving but, the air isn't reaching my lungs. I'm aware of Xavier's arms around me, but even that is not enough to calm me. Growing up around the Motown gang, I thought I'd seen it all, but nothing compares to watching the man you love almost lose his life.

The cops come, Xavier talks to them. They try to speak to me, but I can't think straight enough to even pay attention to what lie Xavier told them. Detroit cops don't care anyway. They have bigger fish to fry than a hotel break-in. It's not until the cops leave and a maintenance man half-ass puts the broken door back on its hinges that I feel like I can breathe normally again.

"You're starting to scare me, baby," Xavier says, finally sitting down on the couch next to me. He pulls me onto his lap, and I curl against him. He's here, he's alive, and I'm alive; we're okay.

"Don't ever fucking scare me like that again," I say quietly.

"I'm sorry."

The room goes quiet except for the sound of us breathing. I take pleasure in the sound. An hour ago, I didn't know if this was going to be possible.

"You're pregnant," he says, his hand going to my stomach.

I smile up at him and shake my head. "I thought I might be, but I'm not. I was just late."

He raises an eyebrow in surprise.

"But it had me thinking about us. What if I was pregnant? We haven't been careful at all. Is that something you want?"

He shrugs. "I haven't thought about it, but I can't lie and say I wasn't a little excited at the thought."

I nod. "When I thought I might be, I was terrified. I can't raise a baby in Detroit, and our relationship isn't exactly solid."

"Then let's fix that."

"What?" I ask. Is he saying what I think he is?

"You haven't seen my world. We've been living in yours. We have to be in Boston tonight anyway."

"I can't leave Sierra."

"Then she'll come with us."

"You have a house?" I ask.

He nods. I pull my bottom lip between my teeth. I'm leaving everything behind for the unknown. The only thing I'm certain about is Xavier.

"What's going to happen when that Alek guy finds out I'm not pregnant?" I don't want to go to Boston if Xavier is going to get killed there.

"We'll cross that bridge when we get to it."

I take a deep breath. This is a huge risk, but the alternative is staying in Detroit, where there's nothing here for me besides Sierra. If Sierra would be honest with herself, she knows there's nothing for her either. Our family was once here, but they're gone, and Ruthless is never coming back.

"I'll book a flight. It will be red-eye. I'll drive you back home so you can talk with Sierra and pack."

I nod my head.

*****

Gravel crunches under the tires as we pull up to a three-story colonial-style house. I've only seen homes like this on TV. I glance in the backseat at Sierra, her eyes widen a fraction, but that's the only indication she gives that she's impressed. Convincing Sierra to come to Boston was about as difficult as I expected. Once I told her that I was leaving whether she came or not, she finally caved. She hates the idea of being at someone else's mercy. I understand, and I have no doubt that she'll be out looking for a job tomorrow morning. The difference here is that she'll be able to find something pretty quick, unlike Detroit.

Xavier puts the car into park right outside the concrete steps that lead up to a big porch. We all exit the car.

"It should be unlocked. Get comfortable. I'll get the bags," Xavier says.

It's close to five in the morning, so the sun is just starting to come up. I turn around to take Sierra's hand. Her curly hair is wild and frizzy from the plane ride, and her eyes have small bags underneath them. She gives me a sad smile, and then we make our way into the house. As soon as we step inside, we both freeze. It's beautiful. Shiny hardwood floors, crisp white walls, there's an area next to the door for people to hang jackets and take off their shoes. French doors open up to what looks like a dining room. Just from the entrance, I can tell the home was completely renovated. Someone who cared about the history of the house did their best to preserve it.

"Holy shit," Sierra breathes.

"Yeah..." I agree.

Xavier comes up behind us, and we move to the side so he can set the bags down.

"Master bedroom is on the top floor at the end of the hall. Besides my office, all the other rooms are empty, so choose what you like, Sierra."

"Thank you," she says.

I squeeze her hand, and we walk off, leaving Xavier to finish unpacking the car. We're both speechless as we explore the house. Every inch of it is beautiful, but I can't help noticing the lack of personal belongings. There are no pictures on the wall or decorations. It looks more like a model home.

"I want this one," Sierra says after we step into another guest room. It's on the second floor, and it has a big window that gives a perfect view of the backyard. The yard is a decent size with...a pool? It's covered with a blue tarp that is lightly dusted with snow.

"Damn, I wish it was summer."

Everything feels so surreal. This is the world I write about in my books, not something that happens. Girls like me don't get saved by Prince Charming.

Sierra yawns and takes a seat on the bed.

"I'll let you sleep," I say.

She gives me a nod. I shut the door and walk back out to the hallway. I walk up the stairs to the top floor and into the last room, where Xavier said the master bedroom is. To my surprise, the room isn't bright and white like the rest of the house. Black-out curtains cover the large windows. The black bedding is unmade. There's a large dresser on one side, and a TV mounted on the wall. It's a big room, but it's dark and plain.

"I usually just sleep here."

I jump at the sound of his deep voice behind me. He walks inside and sets my bags down at the end of the bed. His muscles bunch together under his long sleeve shirt as he does. He never seems to wear a coat, and it's probably because his body runs hot. He's like a damn furnace when we sleep together. Now we'll be sleeping together every night.

"Why?" I ask.

"I take on a lot of jobs."

"Killing jobs?"

He nods, and a sense of sadness washes over me. He was only in Detroit for so long because he was supposed to kill me. Now he'll have other jobs he'll need to leave for.

"You're overthinking," he says, leaning down to place a kiss on my forehead. "Take a shower and get some sleep. I'll be back."

"Where are you going?"

"I have to talk to Alek."

Carmen

I'm not able to fall asleep once Sierra is in her room and Xavier is gone. I walk around the house, still trying to take everything in. There's a lot of things that are up in the air right now, but one thing I know for sure is that I want to be here with Xavier. I want to build a family here. I picture Xavier as a father, and it makes me smile. Then, I remember the mafia he's a part of. It should scare me enough to run, but where would I run to? My life before was more dangerous than the one I want to live with Xavier. My heart is full, no matter how fucked or crazy it might sound. I find a notebook and a pen and settle into the couch to do some writing.

Sierra finally wakes up around noon, and we talk for a while. The fridge is fully stocked, so we make lunch and dinner together. When Xavier isn't back by dinner, I start to worry, but my body is so tired I can't stay up any longer.

"Go to sleep," Sierra tells me. "I'm sure he'll wake you up when he gets home."

Too exhausted to argue with her, I go into the master bedroom, change into pajamas and fall asleep surrounded by his familiar scent.

Shouting from the lower levels of the house wakes me out of my sleep. From the gap in the black-out curtains, I can see that it's still dark outside. The voices get quieter, but I can still hear them. I throw on some socks before rushing down the hall and the two flights of stairs until I can hear the voice more clearly.

"Here are the sleeping pills Doc told you to take," a male voice says. I don't recognize it, but as I come around the corner, I gasp. Xavier is sitting on the couch, but I can barely recognize him.

Both of his eyes are swollen shut, and he's covered in bruises. He can't even sit up straight on the cushion. He's leaned over in an awkward position. Tears instantly fill my eyes.

"Xavier," I gasp, and everyone looks over at me. There's a man, nearly the same size and build, standing over Xavier. Sierra is further away from them with her arms crossed over her chest and a scowl on her face. I reach out to touch Xavier, but every inch of him looks like he's in pain.

"What happened?" I sob, thoroughly embarrassing myself, but I don't care. No one wants to see the person they love like this.

"It's okay, baby," Xavier says. I don't believe him. Nothing about this looks okay.

"It was his punishment," the man behind me says.

"Punishment?!" Sierra and I both ask simultaneously, looking at the man like he's grown two heads. He has short, jet black hair and a chiseled jaw.

He nods. "Xavier went against direct orders. He told Alek that you're here to stay. This is the price he pays."

"What kind of fucked up shit is that?" Sierra asks.

The man shrugs. "It's how things work in the Bratva. Just be happy that he's alive."

I glance at Sierra. The shock and disappointment are evident on her face.

"Is he going to be alright?"

"Yes," both Xavier and the man say at the same time.

"We took him to our Doc. He has a few broken ribs. He's hurt pretty bad, but he should be fine in about a week."

That gives me a little bit of relief but not much considering the way he looks right now. "Here," The man takes out two prescription bottles from his pockets and sets them on the coffee table. "One is a sleeping pill, and the other is a pain pill. He's already had both, so don't give him anything until morning."

I nod.

The man walks out the front door, leaving the three of us alone. Xavier starts to snore loudly, probably the effect of his sleeping pill. I wipe the tears from my face. He's okay.

"You know who else had to deal with this kind of thing? Mom. Is that how you want to end up?"

I know Sierra is just being the big sister, but now is not the time.

"'That's not the same," I reply. I don't have the energy to argue with her right now.

"Why because Xavier is rich?"

Well, that stung. "No, because Xavier isn't Dad. He's not a street thug obsessed with money and unable to care for anyone else. He looks like this because he went against his organization to save me. He would have died for me. Dad would have never done that for mom."

We stare at each other, Sierra's face unchanging.

"It's your life, but I'll be gone as soon as I can."

She turns and walks away. I wonder if she'll ever forgive me for this. Our life will be better now if only she could see it.

"Carmen," Xavier whispers, taking me by surprise. I thought he was asleep.

"Shh, go to sleep," I say.

"Lay with him," he grunts out. His face twists in pain as he moves to a full laying position.

I shake my head. "Your hurt. I don't want to-"

"Lay with me," he demands.

"Stubborn man," I grumble.

Luckily the couch is massive enough to fit both of us, so I lay down in front of him. I try to give him space so I don't touch any of his hurt areas, but he isn't having any of that. He wraps his arms around me and pulls me close to his body.

"Xavier," I scold.

"I'm fine," he says even though he's anything but fine. "This was all worth it to have you right here with me."

"And what's going to happen when they find out I'm not pregnant."

"They already know. I figured I should tell them while I was getting my ass beat to get it all over with at once. I broke the rules, so I endured my punishment. It's over now."

A single tear runs down my face, and I wipe it away.

"Sierra thinks I'm stupid for loving a man like you," I admit.

"What do you think?"

"I feel safe with you. For the first time in my life, I'm not completely on my own. When I'm with you, it feels right, like this is exactly where I'm supposed to be."

He nods. "Then that means this is exactly where you're supposed to be."

****

It takes a little over a week for Xavier to heal. He complained the whole time and tried to convince me that he was fine, stubborn man. Sierra has been relatively quiet the entire time. She's left the house a lot. I assume to look for jobs. Xavier makes sure to have someone drive her wherever she wants to go. He didn't have staff before we moved in, but he has fully staffed the house with security, a housekeeper, and a driver during his time on bed rest. Since he'll still have to leave occasionally to complete jobs, he wanted to make sure I was safe at the house.

He had to show up for a couple of meetings for the Bratva, but besides that, we've both been hiding out at his house like we're on a honeymoon.

"I want to show you something," he says while we sit across from each other at the table.

"What?"

He stands and holds his hand out. "Come on."

I slip my hand into his and let him lead me to the second floor to a door that's been kept locked since we moved in.

He takes a key from his pocket and unlocks it. I look up at him questionably before walking inside. It's a library, but the shelves are empty. There's space for a desk and a chair but not much else.

"I had the shelves installed while you were at the store the other day. I figured you could make this your writing spot. I see you writing all over the house, and I thought it might be good to have a place that's just yours."

I'm speechless, utterly speechless. I walk further into the room, touching the smooth wooden shelves. I could spend hours here writing and reading. These shelves could be full of all my favorite books.

"You don't have to use it. I just thought-"

"I love it," I say as I wrap my arms around his neck and press my lips to his. I've refused to engage in any of Xavier's sex tactics over the last week due to his injuries, but now that he's healed, I jump to wrap my legs around him.

"This is the rest of our life. This house, my library, Boston, the mafia."

He nods. "The rest of our lives."

THE END

Notes

I hope you enjoyed reading *Loving the Bratva*. Please consider leaving a review of this book. Reviews mean the world to indie authors.

Are you curious about Ruthless's story? Check out Golden Handcuffs

Golden Handcuffs

Desperation makes you blind to danger, but I could never be blind to a man like Ruthless.

He runs Detroit, keeping it on the list of the most dangerous cities in the country.

I have to get out of this city. Ruthless is my escape plan.

I just hope I don't get killed in the process.

Golden Handcuffs, *noun,* A situation that is undesirable, unenjoyable, or unfulfilling but that provides enough financial security as to make one unable to leave.

ALSO BY K.D CLARK

Merciless Queen

Cassandra doesn't need a Prince Charming.

She has saved herself more times than she can count.

Life as the Boss of the biggest criminal organization in North America is not an easy job but maybe for one night she can forget about all that.

When she runs into a handsome man in her nightclub she doesn't ask any questions because she couldn't care less.

Cassandra is a boss but so is Andre and he's about to show her that he can be just as ruthless as her.

Savage Spades

The last thing Cam needs right now is the town's motorcycle club taking over her bar.

The failing bar that her father left her to deal with along with a loan from a dangerous man named Venom.

On top of that, she's trying to get through her classes without failing.

She doesn't have time for the blue-eyed monster of a man that can't keep his eyes off her.

But damn he would be a good distraction.

Dirty Empire

I married a monster.

Years ago my husband was the perfect man, until I was faced with his abusive side. I thought my husband would kill me but Maverick saved me. He seemed like my knight in shining armor. However, Maverick comes with his own set of baggage.

How will this tangled web of destruction and lust unravel?

Dirty Empire will thrill, anger, push, and prod you to the edges of your imagination!

King of The Bronx

He belongs to the most notorious criminal organization in North America.

I watched him kill a man without blinking.

I've let him into my heart, and now I'm about to be his next target.

I need thirty-thousand dollars to save the only family I have, and the only way I know how to get it is by stealing from Enzo Genovese.

About the Author

K.D Clark started reading romance books way too young. Now she's a professional at writing books about bad men with hearts of gold. When she's not absorbed in her latest book, she can be found eating tacos alongside a strawberry margarita, reading, or talking to her dogs. Follow her on Tiktok, Instagram, or FB to keep up with her latest news.

Website

https://kdclark926116107.wordpress.com/

Instagram

https://www.instagram.com/authork.dclark/

Facebook

https://www.facebook.com/AuthorKDClark/

TikTok

https://www.tiktok.com/@authork.dclark?lang=en